340648

Mousse Flute

Andrew Matthews

BONNYRIGG

D1464669

Midlothian Libraries

900340648 9

Blue Bananas

To Rob and Carys
A.M.

For Jeremy Lloyd
V.J-O.

Mouse Flute

Andrew Matthews

340648

Vanessa Julian-Ottie

MAMMOTH

Titles in the series:

Big Dog and Little Dog Visit the Moon
The Nut Map
Dilly and the Goody-Goody
Tom's Hats
Juggling with Jeremy
Baby Bear Comes Home
The Magnificent Mummies
Mouse Flute
Delilah Digs for Treasure
Owl in the House
Runaway Fred
Keeping Secrets

First published in Great Britain 1997
by Heinemann and Mammoth, imprints of Reed International Books Ltd
Michelin House, 81 Fulham Road, London SW3 6RB
and Auckland, Melbourne, Singapore and Toronto
Text copyright © Andrew Matthews 1997
Illustrations copyright © Vanessa Julian-Ottie 1997
The moral right of the author and illustrator has been asserted
Paperback ISBN 0 7497 2634 2
Hardback ISBN 0 434 97462 5
1 3 5 7 9 10 8 6 4 2
A CIP catalogue record for this title
is available from the British Library
Produced by Mandarin Offset Ltd
Printed and bound in China
This book is sold subject to the condition
that it shall not, by way of trade or otherwise,
be lent, resold, hired out, or otherwise circulated
without the publisher's prior consent in any form
of binding or cover other than that in which
it is published and without a similar condition
including this condition being imposed
on the subsequent purchaser.

Mouse looked out of his window at
the morning. There were clouds in
the sky, but the sun was shining. It did
not look warm, but it did not look cold.

5

The wind blew hard. It rattled Mouse's window panes and whistled down his chimney-pot. It blew under the door and all round the house.

'I know where Spring is,' said Mouse.

Mouse put on his scarf and his
backpack and went down the road
to Bear's house. Bear was leaning
on the gate yawning.

How are you today, Bear?

Yawn. Yawn. I don't know.

'It isn't Winter and it
isn't Spring,' said Bear.
'I can't tell if I'm awake or asleep.'

Mouse walked on down the road until

he came to Weasel's house.

Weasel was standing at the door with

a broom in his paws.

'I want to Spring-clean my house,'

said Weasel. 'But when will it be Spring?'

'Soon,' said Mouse.

Mouse went into the wood.

It was dim and still.

He put down his pack

and took out

his flute.

He stood on a log and closed
his eyes. All the quiet
gathered in Mouse's
ears until he knew
how to make
the music
of Spring.

Mouse played his flute. The notes
rippled through the air.
Everything in the wood
began to wake.

The sun filled the wood with light.
The trees put out leaves and
whispered their Winter
dreams to the wind.

Flowers pushed up through the earth.

Birds began to build nests.

Everything moved in time to the

glittering sound of Mouse's flute.

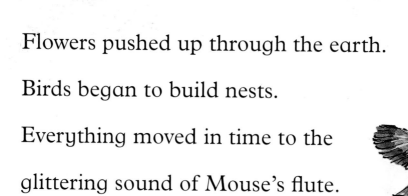

Mouse stopped playing.

He opened his eyes and smiled.

Then he put away his flute and walked

home through the warm Spring day.

When Mouse reached Weasel's house,

Weasel had already swept the floor

and polished the table and chairs.

Now he was cleaning the windows.

'Have a rest,' Mouse called.

'Come to my house for a snack.'

Soon after, Bear came along,

carrying a jar of honey.

'Come to my house for

lunch, Weasel,' he said.

Weasel worked all morning.

The warm sun made the other animals

sleepy. They snoozed in the shade.

Weasel went on working.

18

Weasel raced round the garden
pulling up weeds. He dug holes.
He planted seeds until he was tired
and giddy.

19

Later, Mouse and Bear decided to go

on a picnic. 'Come with us,' they called

to Weasel. But he was still busy.

20

Mouse smiled to himself.

He took his flute from his

pack and began to play.

The music was slow and
deep, like a flowing river.
It sparkled like sunlight on water.
Weasel dropped his spade
and went to listen.

23

The three friends walked to the river.
They ate their picnic. Then they sat
on the river bank and dipped their
hot paws in the cool water.

Oh my, this is fun!

When it was evening they all went
home together. Mouse played his flute.
The stars came out to listen.

Bear and Weasel hummed along
and the three friends walked
home in the starlight.

27

Summer came at last and the

three friends had many picnics

in the hot sun and Mouse

played his flute.

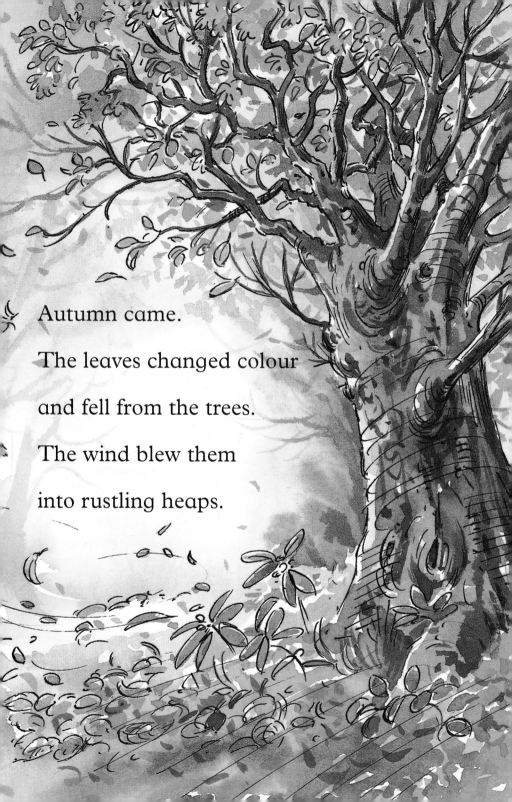

Autumn came.

The leaves changed colour
and fell from the trees.
The wind blew them
into rustling heaps.

Then Winter came.

It froze puddles white

and stuck icicles on twigs.

It drew swirly shapes on the windows.

It was nearly Christmas.

Bear invited Mouse and Weasel to dinner.

Bear.
The Lodge

Please come to
my house for dinner
on Christmas Day.
love
Bear.

Bear had presents for his friends.

There was a new scarf for Mouse

and a soft duster for Weasel.

Bear wrapped them as

neatly as he could.

He looked round the

room and frowned.

'This place needs

cheering up,' he said.

Bear made chains from strips of brightly coloured paper. He put up Christmas cards on every shelf and hung tinsel and angels over the door. But something was missing.

Something's missing – I wonder what?

33

Bear scratched his head and sucked his paw. He thought hard about what was missing. At last he knew.

Bear looked through the window.

It was dark outside.

It was snowing. Snowflakes twirled

in the air. A cold wind moaned

through the trees.

Bear put on his cap.

He picked up a lantern

and a small, sharp axe.

He walked out into

the wood. The first

tree he saw was

too tall to take

indoors.

You're too big
for my room.

Bear walked on until he came to a

small fir tree but the branches were

too wide to go through his door.

Bear walked on until he came to

another tree. It was not too tall.

It was not too wide.

Bear put down the lantern.

He lifted the axe to cut the tree.

But the little tree shook.

All right, little tree!
I won't cut you down.

It trembled so much that all

the snow tumbled from

its branches.

Bear felt so sorry for the tree that

he did not cut it down. He walked

home and went straight to bed.

When Bear woke up, it was
Christmas Day. Mouse and Weasel
came to Bear's house carrying their
Christmas presents.

They looked round Bear's room.

Where's the Christmas tree, Bear?

'I nearly got a Christmas tree,'

Bear said sadly, 'but I felt sorry for it.

I didn't want to cut it down so I left it

where it was.'

Mouse smiled.

He took out his

flute and played.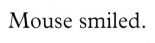

It was a Christmas tune.

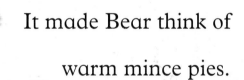

It made Bear think of

warm mince pies.

It made Weasel think of

holly and Christmas pudding.

Bear began to dance.

His heavy feet made the room shake.

Tinsel and paper chains fell off

the wall and dropped on

Bear's shoulders.

More tinsel!

'Bear looks just like a Christmas tree!'

said Weasel. 'Let's turn him into one!'

They wound more tinsel round Bear.

They put an angel on his head

and piled presents at his feet.

MIDLOTHIAN COUNCIL LIBRARY

48